ANNA BANANA

ANNA BANANA

101 JUMP-ROPE RHYMES

COMPILED BY

JOANNA COLE

ILLUSTRATED BY

ALAN TIEGREEN

A Beech Tree Paperback Book
New York

Library of Congress Cataloging in Publication Data
Cole, Joanna. Anna Banana: 101 jump-rope rhymes / Joanna Cole: illustrated
by Alan Tiegreen. p. cm. Bibliography: p. Includes index.
Summary: An illustrated collection of jump rope rhymes arranged according
to the type of jumping they are meant to accompany. 1. Counting-out rhymes.
2. Jump rope rhymes. 3. Children—Folklore. [1. Jump rope rhymes. 2. Games.]
I. Tiegreen, Alan, ill. II. Title. GR485.C65 1989 398'.8—dc19 88-29108 CIP AC
ISBN 0-688-08809-0
23 24 25 26 27 28 29 30
First Beech Tree edition, 1991

FOR JHONEEN

CONTENTS

ANNA BANANA

INTRODUCTION

ABOUT JUMPING ROPE
AND JUMP-ROPE RHYMES

Children have been jumping rope for thousands of years, but for only a fraction of that time have there been jump-rope rhymes. Until about a hundred years ago, jumping rope was a competitive game. Most jumpers were boys, each had his own rope, and the object was to see who could jump the fastest, the highest, or the most times without tripping.

As times changed and girls were encouraged to be more active, the jump rope was gradually taken over by them. Boys did not stop jumping altogether, but girls jumped more, and when boys did jump, they usually joined a group of girls. As a girls' game, jump rope changed in interesting ways.

For instance, although girls sometimes jumped individually, they often jumped in groups, with several girls sharing one long rope. Two girls were the "enders," who turned the rope; the other girls were the jumpers.

There was still competition, for every girl wanted to be the best jumper. But there was also cooperation; the enders had to turn evenly and rhythmically so the jumpers could do their best. Then, when it was the enders' turn to jump, their friends would turn as well for them.

There was another change, too. As girls jumped, they made an art as well as a sport of the game: they invented the jump-rope rhyme. Rhymes helped the enders keep the rhythm, and they also lent poetry and humor to the game.

The subjects of the rhymes are satisfyingly down-to-earth, ranging from the commonplaces of the table ("Two little sausages frying in the pan" or "Jelly in the dish"), to family squabbles and sibling rivalry ("Johnny broke a teacup / And blamed it on me"), to girl meets boy ("Ice cream soda, Delaware punch. / Spell the initials of your honeybunch").

Each rhyme goes with a certain kind of jumping game. Some, such as "Johnny gave me apples, / Johnny gave me pears," mark time for straight jumping; others, like the famous "I'm a little Dutch girl," give directions for actions and stunts to perform while jumping. A whole series of short rhymes serve as introductions for simply counting the number of jumps; examples of these are the well-known Cinderella rhymes ("Cinderella dressed in yellow / Went downstairs to kiss her fellow. / How many kisses did she give?"). Other rhymes are for jumping very fast ("pepper"); or for fortune-telling ("Fortune-teller, please tell me"); or for running in and out of the rope ("Callings in and callings out, / I call Rudy in . . ."). I have arranged this book in chapters according to these games, because it is satisfying to think of the rhymes connected so closely to the play that inspired them. Usually the rules for the games are self-evident from the rhymes; when this is not the case, I have added a line or two of instructions.

If you do not find one of your favorite jump-rope rhymes in this collection, it may be because that rhyme is traditionally used in another type of activity. For instance, in some places, children may jump rope to the popular rhyme "A, My Name Is Alice," but that is the exception; it is most often used for ball-bouncing. The humorous verse "Miss Lucy Had a Baby" is likewise not included here because it is almost always a hand-clapping rhyme, as are "Miss Mary Mack" and "Hambone, Hambone." There is, of course, some overlapping among the games, but for the most part, the rhymes you will find in this book are the ones that have generally been used for jumping rope only.

New jump-rope rhymes are always being invented, most of them based on the ones presented here—the traditional rhymes that accompanied the tap of the jump rope on America's sidewalks years ago, and that can still be heard today whenever children are jumping rope.

JUMP-ROPE RHYMES

STRAIGHT JUMPING

Skilled jumpers can do all sorts of fancy tricks and stunts, but often they prefer just plain jumping—with a good rhyme to keep the rhythm going. Here are some favorite rhymes.

—————————△ ▽ △—————————

I went upstairs to make my bed.
I made a mistake and bumped my head.
I went downstairs to milk my cow.
I made a mistake and milked the sow.
I went in the kitchen to bake a pie.
I made a mistake and baked a fly.

Standing on the corner
Chewing bubble gum.
Along came a beggar
And asked me for some.

Standing at the bar
Smoking a cigar.
Laughing at the donkey
Ha—ha—har!

Tomatoes, lettuce, carrots, peas.
Mother said you have to eat a lot of these.

Ice cream, a penny a lump.
The more you eat—the more you jump!

As I was walking near the lake,
I met a little rattlesnake.
He ate so much of jelly-cake,
It made his little belly ache.

I won't go to Macy's anymore, more, more.
There's a big fat policeman at the door, door, door.
He grabs me by the collar
And makes me pay a dollar,
So I won't go to Macy's anymore, more, more.

My boyfriend's name is Billy.
He is so silly-silly.
He has forty-nine toes
And a pickle for a nose,
And that's the way the story goes.

Cups and saucers,
Plates and dishes.
My old man wears
Calico britches.

Yellow-belly, yellow-belly, come and take a swim.
Yes, by golly, when the tide comes in.

A sailor went to sea sea sea
To see what he could see see see.
But all that he could see see see,
Was the bottom of the deep blue sea sea sea.

One, two, three, four, five, six, seven.
All good children go to heaven.
Seven, six, five, four, three, two, one.
All bad children suck their thumb.

Alice, where are you going?
"Upstairs to take a bath."
Alice with legs like toothpicks
And a neck like a giraffe.
Alice in the bathtub,
Alice pulled the plug.
Oh my goodness, oh my soul,
There goes Alice down the hole!

I love coffee,
I love tea.
I love the boys
And the boys love me.

Postman, postman, do your duty.
Send this letter to an American beauty.
Don't you stop and don't delay.
Get it to her right away.

Johnny gave me apples,
Johnny gave me pears,
Johnny gave me fifty cents
And kissed me on the stairs.
I'd rather wash the dishes,
I'd rather scrub the floor,
I'd rather kiss the iceman
Behind the kitchen door.

Two in the middle and two at the end,
Each is a sister and each is a friend.
A penny to save and a penny to spend,
Two in the middle and two at the end.

**Bluebells, cockle shells,
Eevy, ivy, OVER.**

(This is a slow, singsong rhyme for getting the jumping started. On the first line, the enders swing the rope back and forth near the ground without making a full turn. On the word "over," they swing the rope up and over and start reciting a rhyme.)

"Enders" are the two who turn the rope.

HOW MANY?

It's a challenge to see how many times you can jump without missing. Here are rhymes for counting the number.

—————————— △ ▽ △ ——————————

Chickety, chickety, chop.
How many times before I stop?
One, two, three, four, five, etc.

Candy, candy in the dish.
How many pieces do you wish?
One, two, three, four, five . . .

My mother made a chocolate cake.
How many eggs did it take?
One, two, three, four, five . . .

Hello, hello, hello, sir.
Meet me at the grocer.
No, sir. Why, sir?
Because I have a cold, sir.
Where did you get the cold, sir?
At the North Pole, sir.
What were you doing there, sir?
Counting polar bears, sir.
How many did you count, sir?
One, two, three, four, five . . .

My little sister dressed in pink
Washed all the dishes in the sink.
How many dishes did she break?
One, two, three, four, five . . .

My old granddad made a shoe.
How many nails did he put through?
One, two, three, four, five . . .

Here comes teacher with a great big stick.
I wonder what I got in arithmetic.
One, two, three, four, five . . .

Here comes teacher yelling.
Wonder what I got in spelling.
One, two, three, four, five . . .

Teacher, teacher, oh, so tired.
How many times were you fired?
One, two, three, four, five . . .

Cinderella dressed in yellow
Went downstairs to kiss her fellow.
How many kisses did she give?
One, two, three, four, five . . .

Cinderella dressed in lace
Went upstairs to powder her face.
How many puffs did she use?
One, two, three, four, five . . .

Cinderella dressed in red
Went downstairs to bake some bread.
How many loaves did she bake?
One, two, three, four, five . . .

Cinderella dressed in green
Went upstairs to eat ice cream.
How many spoonfuls did she eat?
One, two, three, four, five . . .

Cinderella dressed in blue
Went outside to tie her shoe.
How many seconds did it take?
One, two, three, four, five . . .

Mother, Mother, I am sick.
Send for the doctor, quick, quick, quick.
Doctor, Doctor, will I die?
Yes, my dear, and so will I.
How many coaches will I have?
One, two, three, four, five . . .

Down in the valley
Where the green grass grows,
There sat Tracy
Sweet as a rose.
She sang, she sang,
She sang so sweet.
Along came Ben
And kissed her cheek.
How many kisses did he give her?
One, two, three, four, five . . .

Down by the river,
Down by the sea.
Mary went fishing
With Daddy and me.
How many fish did Mary get?
One, two, three, four, five . . .

Names that are printed this way—Mary—are the
names of the jumpers and their friends.

Sugar, salt, pepper, cider.
How many legs has a bow-legged spider?
One, two, three, four, five . . .

Charlie Chaplin sat on a pin.
How many inches did it go in?
One, two, three, four, five . . .

Popeye went down in the cellar
To drink some spinach juice.
How many gallons did he drink?
One, two, three, four, five . . .

Tell me, tell me, tell me true.
How old, how old, how old are you?
One, two, three, four, five . . .

I was born in a frying pan.
Can you guess how old I am?
One, two, three, four, five . . .

RED-HOT PEPPER!

When a rhyme says the words "pepper" or "hot" or "red-hot peas," the enders turn the rope *very fast*, trying to make the jumper miss.

──────────△ ▽ △──────────

Mabel, Mabel, set the table,
Just as fast as you are able.
Don't forget the salt, sugar, vinegar, mustard,
    red-hot *pepper!*

Johnny over the ocean,
Johnny over the sea,
Johnny broke a teacup
And blamed it on me.
I told Ma,
Ma told Pa.
Johnny got in trouble,
Hee, hee, haw!
Salt, vinegar,
Mustard, *pepper!*

Old Man Lazy
Drives me crazy.
Up the ladder,
Down the ladder,
H-O-T spells *hot!*

(On "up the ladder," the
jumper moves toward
one of the enders; on
"down the ladder," she
jumps toward the other.)

Up and down the ladder wall,
Penny loaf to feed us all.
I buy milk, you buy flour,
You shall have *pepper* **in half an hour.**

I told Mama
And Mama told Papa
And Papa told Mama
To give me some *red-hot peas!*

Mother sent me to the store.
This is what she sent me for:
To get some coffee, tea, and *pepper.*

ACTIONS

Can you reach down and touch the ground while jumping? These rhymes ask you to do all kinds of things without missing a beat.

—————————————△ ▽ △—————————————

I'm a little Dutch girl
Dressed in blue.
Here are the things
I like to do:
Salute to the captain,
Bow to the queen,
Turn my back
on the submarine.
I can do the tap dance,
I can do the split,
I can do the holka polka
Just like this.

Spanish dancer, do the split.
Spanish dancer, give a kick.
Spanish dancer, turn around.
Spanish dancer, get out of town.

(On the last line, the jumper runs out.)

Teddy bear, teddy bear,
Turn around.
Teddy bear, teddy bear,
Touch the ground.
Teddy bear, teddy bear,
Show your shoe.
Teddy bear, teddy bear,
That will do.
Teddy bear, teddy bear,
Go upstairs.
Teddy bear, teddy bear,
Say your prayers.
Teddy bear, teddy bear,
Turn out the light.
Teddy bear, teddy bear,
Say good night.

Apple on a stick,
Five cents a lick.
Every time I turn around
It makes me sick.

Benjamin Franklin went to France
To teach the ladies how to dance.
First the heel, and then the toe,
Spin around and out you go.

Jelly in the dish,
Jelly in the dish.
Wiggle, waggle, wiggle, waggle.
Jelly in the dish.

Bubble gum, bubble gum, chew and blow.
Bubble gum, bubble gum, scrape your toe.
Bubble gum, bubble gum, tastes so sweet.
Get that bubble gum off your feet!

Two little sausages frying in the pan.
One went POP and the other went BANG!

(Two players jump together. On the word "pop," one player jumps out on one side. On the word "bang," the other player jumps out on the other side.)

**Down the Mississippi
Where the boats go PUSH!**

(Players stand in line, and on the word "push," the first player is pushed into the rope. The rhyme is repeated, and on the second "push," the second player is pushed in; the two jump together, and on the next "push," the second player pushes the first player out, etc., etc.)

When it rains, the Mississippi River
Gets higher, higher, higher, and higher!

(The enders hold the rope taut about an inch off the ground. Players line up to jump over the rope, which is gradually raised.)

The clock stands still
While the hands go around.
One o'clock, two o'clock . . .

(One player jumps in place, while another jumps around her in a circle, counting up to "twelve o'clock.")

Fudge, fudge, tell the judge,
Mama's got a newborn baby.
It isn't a girl and it isn't a boy,
It's just a fair young lady.
Wrap it up in tissue paper.
Send it up the elevator.
First floor, miss.
Second floor, miss.
Third floor, miss.
Fourth floor, miss.
Fifth floor, miss.
Sixth floor, baby's floor.
All out!

(On the "floors," the enders raise the rope gradually and turn it so that it doesn't touch the ground.
This stunt is called "High Waters.")

Little white rabbit,
    hop on one foot, one foot.
Little white rabbit,
    hop on two feet, two feet.
Little white rabbit,
    hop on three feet, three feet.
Little white rabbit,
    hop on no feet, no feet.

(On "three feet," the jumper puts one hand to the
ground. On "no feet," she runs out.)

Oliver jump
Oliver jump jump jump.
Oliver kick
Oliver kick kick kick.
Oliver twist
Oliver twist twist twist.
Oliver jump jump jump.
Oliver kick kick kick.
Oliver twist twist twist.

Dolly Dimple walks like this,
Dolly Dimple talks like this,
Dolly Dimple smiles like this,
Dolly Dimple throws a kiss.

Blondie and Dagwood went to town.
Blondie bought an evening gown.
Dagwood bought a pair of shoes.
Cookie stayed home to watch the news.
And this is what it said:
"Close your eyes and count to ten.
If you miss, you take an end."

Anna Banana
Played the piano.
All she knew was "The Star-Spangled Banner."
Banana, banana split.

NOW'S THE TIME TO MISS

When the enders chant a rhyme about missing, they may speed up and try to make the jumper trip. Or the jumper herself may miss on purpose. She can choose to step on the rope, put a foot on either side of it, stand still, or just run out.

△ ▽ △

Andy, Mandy,
Sugar candy,
Now's the time to *miss!*

Jump rope, jump rope,
Will I miss?
Jump rope, jump rope,
Just watch this!

Miss, miss, little miss, miss.
When she misses, she misses like this.

I know a woman
And her name is Miss.
And all of a sudden
She goes like—this.

I know a man, his name is Mister.
He knows a lady, and her name is MISS.

Little Miss Pinky, dressed in blue,
Died last night at half-past two.
Before she died, she told me this,
"Let the jump rope miss like this."

YES, NO, MAYBE SO . . .

Some rhymes ask a question followed by a
list of possible answers. The choice may be a
simple "yes, no, yes, no," or it may be a list
of colors, houses, or numbers. The word you
happen to miss on is the answer.

———————————△ ▽ △———————————

My ma and your ma were
    hanging out the clothes.
My ma gave your ma
    a punch in the nose.
Did it hurt her?
Yes, no, maybe so, yes, no, maybe so . . .

My little girl, dressed in blue,
Died last night at half-past two.
Did she go up or down?
Up, down, up, down, up, down . . .

What shall I name my little pup?
I'll have to think a good one up.
A, B, C, D, E, F, G . . .

(When the jumper misses, she makes up a name
beginning with that letter.)

Sam, Sam, **do you love** Julie?
Yes, no, yes, no, yes, no . . .

Annie, Annie, **do you love** Ben?
Yes, no, yes, no, yes, no . . .

Names that are printed this way—Mary—are the
names of the jumpers and their friends.

ABC's and vegetable goop.
What will I find in the alphabet soup?
A, B, C, D, E, F, G . . .

(The player makes up something that starts with
the letter on which she misses. Often it's something
funny.)

Here is a question-and-answer rhyme that tells
your fortune:

Will I marry?
Yes, no, yes, no, yes, no . . .

Where will the wedding be?
Church, synagogue, house, barn,
Church, synagogue, house, barn . . .

What color suit will your husband wear?
Red, blue, black, green,
Red, blue, black, green . . .

How many children will you have?
One, two, three, four, five . . .

Will your children behave themselves?
Yes, no, yes, no, yes, no . . .

TELL ME THE NAME OF YOUR SWEETHEART

There are lots of fortune-telling rhymes that predict only one thing: the first letter of your future sweetheart's name.

———————————— △ ▽ △ ————————————

Strawberry, apple, my jam tart.
Tell me the name of your sweetheart.
A, B, C, D, E, F, G . . .

Raspberry, raspberry, raspberry jam.
What are the initials of my young man?
A, B, C, D, E, F, G . . .

Strawberry shortcake, cream on top.
Tell me the name of my sweetheart.
A, B, C, D, E, F, G . . .

Apples, peaches, creamery butter.
Here's the name of my true lover.
A, B, C, D, E, F, G . . .

Ice cream soda, Delaware punch.
Spell the initials of your honeybunch.
A, B, C, D, E, F, G . . .

Fortune-teller, please tell me
What my husband's name will be.
A, B, C, D, E, F, G . . .

Red, white, and blue,
Stars shine over you.
Red, white, and yellow,
Who is your fellow?
Red, white, and pink,
Who do you think?
A, B, C, D, E, F, G . . .

IN AND OUT

Jumping in and out of the rope is fun—if you can do it gracefully. Many in-and-out rhymes let the jumper call in a friend by name.

—————————△ ▽ △—————————

Rooms for rent,
Inquire within.
As I move out
Let Rachel come in.

In, spin.
Let Laura come in.
Out, spout.
Let Laura go out.

I love coffee, I love tea,
I want Amy to come in with me.

Oh, in I run and around I go,
Clap my hands and nod just so.
I lift my knee and slap my shoe.
When I go out, let Ginny come in.

Callings in and callings out,
I call Rudy in.
Rudy's in and won't go out—
I call Kathie in.

Dancing Dolly had no sense.
She bought a fiddle for eighteen cents.
But the only tune that she could play
Was "Alex, get out of the donkey's way!"

(On the last line, "Alex" jumps out, and a new
jumper comes in.)

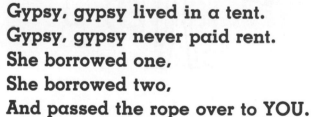

California oranges, fifty cents a pack.
Come on, Donna, and tap me on the back.

(At the end of the verse, "Donna" jumps in and
taps the jumper, who then jumps out.)

Gypsy, gypsy lived in a tent.
Gypsy, gypsy never paid rent.
She borrowed one,
She borrowed two,
And passed the rope over to YOU.

**Every morning at eight o'clock,
You all may hear the postman's knock.
One, two, three, four. There goes** Stephanie
out the door.

("Stephanie" runs out, another player jumps in,
and the verse is repeated.)

**Keep the kettle boiling.
Don't be late!**

(Jumpers stand in a line, and, one after the other,
each runs in to the rope, jumps out on the other
side, and returns to the end of the line.)

Not last night but the night before,
Twenty-four robbers came knocking at my door.
As I ran out, they ran in.
I hit them on the head with a rolling pin.

(On "I ran out," the jumper jumps out; on "they
ran in," she jumps in again.)

A B C D E F G,
H I J K L M N O P,
Q R S T U *are out!*

Changing bedrooms number 1.
Changing bedrooms number 2.
Changing bedrooms number 3 . . .

(Jumpers run in from each side, changing places
with one another on each number.)

ALL IN TOGETHER

When there are five or six players, everyone can jump at once.

——————————△ ▽ △——————————

All in together, girls.
How do you like the weather, girls?
January, February, March, April . . .

(Each jumper runs in when she hears the month of her birthday. Then the months are repeated, and each girl jumps out on her birthday month.)

Sheep in the meadow,
Cows in the corn.
Jump in on the month that you were born.
January, February, March, April . . .

Everybody, everybody,
Come on in.
The first one misses
Must take my end.

All in, a bottle of gin.
All out, a bottle of stout.

Five, ten, fifteen, twenty.
Do not leave the jump rope empty.

WHERE TO FIND MORE

SOME SOURCES FOR JUMP-ROPE RHYMES

Abrahams, Roger D., ed. *Jump Rope Rhymes: A Dictionary*. Published for the American Folklore Society. Austin: University of Texas Press, 1969.

Ainsworth, Catherine Harris. "Jump Rope Verses Around the United States." *Western Folklore*, Vol. 20 (1961), pp. 179–99.

Babcock, W. H. "Games of Washington Children." *American Anthropologist*, Vol. 1 (1888), pp. 266–68.

Botkin, B. A. *A Treasury of American Folklore*. New York: Crown, 1944.

Emrich, Duncan. *The Hodge Podge Book*. New York: Four Winds Press, 1972. (See also *The Nonsense Book*, 1970, and *The Whim-Wham Book*, 1975.)

Gomme, Alice B. *The Traditional Games of England, Scotland, and Ireland*. 2 vols. London, 1894–98. Reprinted: New York: Dover, 1964.

Knapp, Herbert and Mary. *One Potato, Two Potato . . . The Secret Education of American Children.* New York: W. W. Norton, 1976.

Morrison, Lillian, comp. *A Diller, A Dollar.* New York: Thomas Y. Crowell, 1955.

Nulton, Lucy. "Jump Rope Rhymes as Folk Literature." *Journal of American Folklore*, Vol. 61 (1948), pp. 53–67.

Opie, Iona and Peter. *The Lore and Language of School Children.* Oxford: Clarendon Press, 1959.

Withers, Carl. *A Rocket in My Pocket.* New York: Holt, 1948.

Yoffie, Leah Rachel Clara. "Three Generations of Singing Games in St. Louis." *Journal of American Folklore*, Vol. 60 (1947), pp. 1–51.

INDEX OF FIRST LINES